Wings!

clings.

Flings...

Stings.

Dings...

Things.

Brings?

Springs....

Sings!

Rings!

Zings!

WINGS

Written by
Cheryl B. Klein

Illustrated by
Tomie dePaola

Atheneum Books for Young Readers
New York   London   Toronto   Sydney   New Delhi

For James and the nest we've built together
—C. B. K.

For Mary Ellen and Don Olson
—T. deP.

ATHENEUM BOOKS FOR YOUNG READERS
An imprint of Simon & Schuster Children's Publishing Division
1230 Avenue of the Americas, New York, New York 10020
Text copyright © 2019 by Cheryl B. Klein
Illustrations copyright © 2019 by Tomie dePaola

ATHENEUM BOOKS FOR YOUNG READERS
is a registered trademark of Simon & Schuster, Inc.
Atheneum logo is a trademark of Simon & Schuster, Inc.
For information about special discounts for bulk purchases,
please contact Simon & Schuster Special Sales at
1-866-506-1949 or business@simonandschuster.com.
The Simon & Schuster Speakers Bureau can bring authors to your
live event. For more information or to book an event, contact
the Simon & Schuster Speakers Bureau at 1-866-248-3049
or visit our website at www.simonspeakers.com.
Book design by Laurent Linn
The text for this book was set in Chaloops Galaxy Normal.
The illustrations were created by collage using Avery full-sheet labels with
markers for the color. The background paper was painted using acrylics.
Manufactured in China
1218 SCP
First Edition
1 2 3 4 5 6 7 8 9 10
Library of Congress Cataloging-in-Publication Data
Names: Klein, Cheryl B., 1978– author. | DePaola, Tomie, 1934–
illustrator.
Title: Wings / Cheryl B. Klein ; Illustrated by Tomie dePaola.
Description: First edition. | New York : Atheneum, [2019] | Summary: Illustrations and simple, rhyming text
follow a baby bird on its first flight,
which starts cautiously, but ends with delight.
Identifiers: LCCN 2017052949 (print) | LCCN 2017061088 (eBook) |
ISBN 9781534405103 (hardcover : alk. paper) | ISBN 9781534405110 (eBook)
Subjects: | CYAC: Stories in rhyme. | Birds—Fiction. | Flight—Fiction.
Classification: LCC PZ8.3.K6573 (eBook) | LCC PZ8.3.K6573 Win 2019 (print) | DDC [E]—dc23
LC record available at https://lccn.loc.gov/2017052949